Dip 1

Written by Sue Graves
Illustrated by Sandra Aguilar

Collins

Sam is at a dip.

3

It nips!

4

Pam dips in.

Pam nips a pad.

6

Pip dips in.

Pip tips in!

Dad dips in.

Dad nips Pip!

12

Dips

Tips

Nips

Ideas for reading

Written by Linda Pagett B.Ed (Hons), M.Ed
Lecturer and Educational Consultant

Learning objectives: link sounds to letters; hear and say sounds in words in the order in which they occur; read simple words by sounding out and blending the phonemes; read texts compatible with phonic knowledge and skills; retell narratives in the correct sequence, drawing on the language patterns of stories

Curriculum links: Personal, Social and Emotional Development: Making relationships

Focus phonemes: s, a, t, p, i, n, m, d

Word count: 28

Getting started

- Revise the focus phonemes with children and practise sounding them out.

- Write the word *dip* on the whiteboard. Model how to sound it out and blend the phonemes to read the word.

- Introduce the book by discussing the illustration on the front cover. Draw children's attention to the characters and what they are doing. Share experiences of fairgrounds and what a lucky dip might be.

- Support children in reading the title and blurb, pointing to the words for support. As a group, predict what the story might be about and what may be found in the bins.

Reading and responding

- Turn to pp2–3 and read the words together, asking children to point to the letters as you sound them out.

- Ask children to read to p13 aloud. Encourage them to blend phonemes to read new words fluently.

- Support children as they read, moving around the group and intervening where necessary to praise, encourage and help.